This edition published by Parragon Books Ltd in 2018 and distributed by

Parragon Inc.
440 Park Avenue South, 13th Floor
New York, NY 10016
www.parragon.com

Text © Hollins University
Illustrations © Parragon Books Ltd 2018

Written by Margaret Wise Brown
Illustrated by Jean Claude

ISBN: 978-1-5270-1805-1

Printed in China

BE
BRAVE,
Little
TIGER!

Parragon

Bath • New York • Cologne • Melbourne • Delhi
Hong Kong • Shenzhen • Singapore

"I'm a brave little tiger, ho ho ho!
I'm not afraid wherever I go!"

A little tiger sang to himself as he walked through the jungle. But the little tiger did not feel brave at all. He was singing to try to convince himself that he *was* brave, but he was afraid of so many things that he **shook** and **shook** with fear.

He was afraid of the **howling** monkeys in the trees, and the **hissing** snakes in the grass.

He was afraid of the **buzzing** bees, and the noise the **wind** made.

He was frightened of the **squawking** birds in the sky...

...and the **jumping** fish in the river.

The other tigers splashed and played in the river every day.

SPLASH!

The little tiger **longed** to join them, but he was too afraid.

"Be brave!" the little tiger's mother said that afternoon,
as she said to him every day. "Nothing is going to hurt you."
But the little tiger still shook and shook.
"Little Tiger, stop shaking or you'll shake your stripes off,"
said his father.

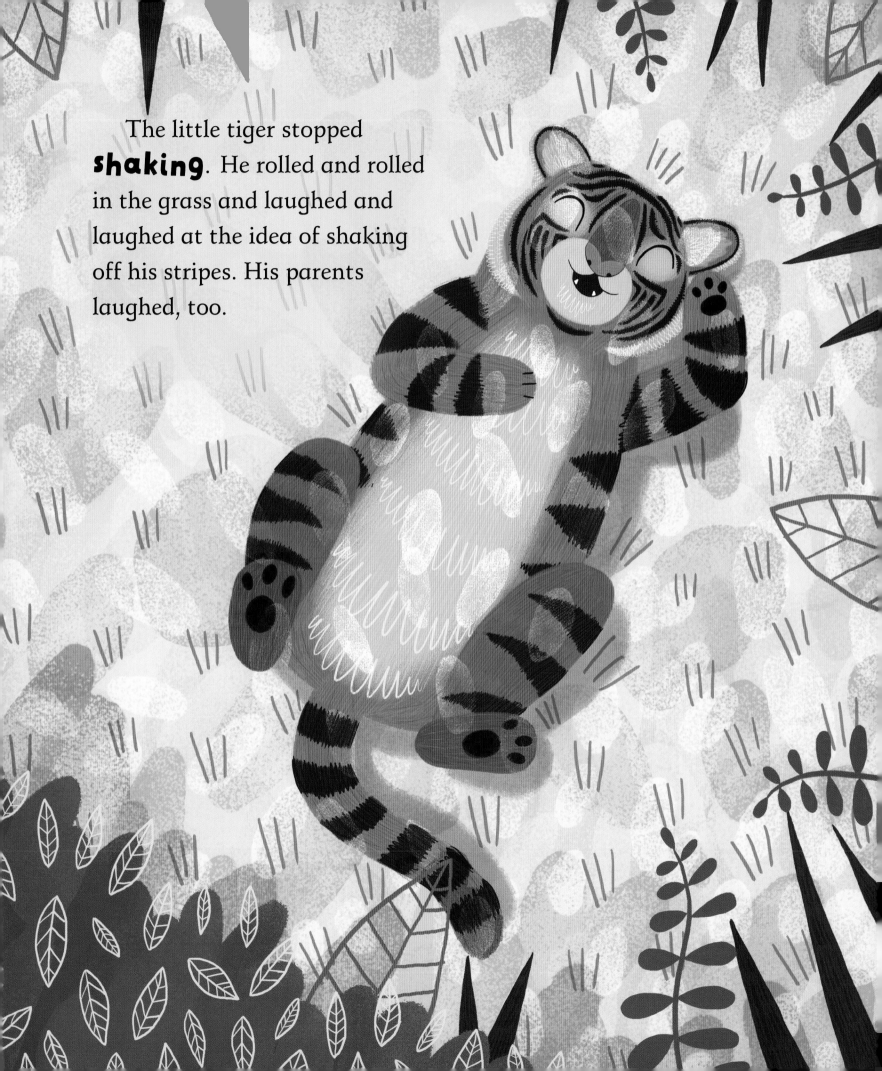

The little tiger stopped **shaking**. He rolled and rolled in the grass and laughed and laughed at the idea of shaking off his stripes. His parents laughed, too.

"Everyone is afraid of something sometimes," said his father.

"Really?" asked the little tiger.

"Yes," said his father. "Even an elephant is afraid sometimes."

The little tiger looked over at a huge elephant fanning his enormous ears and munching on fresh, green grass. How could that great, grave, and gargantuan elephant ever be afraid of anything, the little tiger wondered. Just looking at the elephant made the little tiger start to **shake** again.

Suddenly, a tiny gray mouse skittered its way across the ground right in front of the elephant. The elephant raised his trunk, swished his tail, and galloped off toward the trees.

"**ohhhhh**," said the little tiger as he watched. He stopped shaking and thought about this. The elephant was the biggest animal of all, but it was indeed just like his father said: Even the elephant was afraid of something. And that something happened to be a tiny mouse!

Now it was almost sunset. The little tiger and his
parents walked past the river. They saw tigers lounging
on rocks, warming their backsides with the last rays of
the sun. Soon, they arrived back at the spot in the jungle
where the elephant had encountered the mouse.

The little tiger was surprised to see that the elephant was back. The elephant was delicately plucking one leaf after another off the branches of a banyan tree.

"Did the elephant forget about the mouse? What if the mouse comes back?" the little tiger asked his parents.

"No, the elephant did not forget," said his mother. "Elephants never forget."

"And the elephant knows that the leaves of the banyan tree are among the sweetest and crunchiest leaves in the jungle," she said. "So, even though he remembers that this is where he saw the mouse, he is not letting his fear stop him from doing something he enjoys."

"Ooohhh," said the little tiger as he listened. He thought about this as they walked back home. He also sang his song to himself.

"I'm a brave little tiger, ho ho ho!
I'm not afraid wherever I go!"

He realized he was starting to feel just a *little* brave.

The next morning the little tiger went out for a walk with his parents. They walked past the monkeys in the trees.

Birds flew overhead, bees **buzzed**, and the noisy wind **blew**.

Snakes **slithered** in the grass, and fish **swam** in the river.

The little tiger sang to himself as
the bright, hot sun bathed the jungle.

And you know what?
He felt **MORE** than a *little* brave.

The little tiger felt **very** brave.
He felt *so* brave that he stopped shaking and . . .

SPLASH!